THE F CONTEST

written by Joe Yukish
illustrated by Kate Salley Palmer

KAEDEN BOOKS™

"Hey, Dad!" shouted Matt.
"Let's go fishing," said Kelly.

"I want to go fishing too," said Nick.

"Great idea," said Dad.

"We have a big pontoon boat and fishing poles. We can have a fishing contest."

"Since I do not like to fish, I will sit in the sun," said Mom.

Everyone got into the boat.

Dad drove the boat across the lake.

"We will tell you when you get to a good fishing spot," said Kelly.

Dad continued to drive the boat across the lake.

"Look at the fish jumping!" yelled Matt.

"Here is a good fishing spot!"
yelled Kelly.

"Stop here! Stop here!" yelled Nick.

"This is a good place for me to sit in the sun," said Mom.

Dad put the anchor over the side of the boat. "Let's see who can catch the biggest fish," said Dad.

"I will fish from the front of the boat," said Matt.

"I want to fish from the front too," said Kelly.

"I want to fish from the side," said Dad.

"I will fish from the side with Dad," said Nick.

15

"I will stretch out up here in the sun," said Mom.

Splash!

"That was a big fish," said Matt, "but I didn't catch it."

Splash!

"That was a bigger fish," said Kelly, "but I didn't catch it."

Splash!

"That was the biggest fish," said Nick, "but I didn't catch it."

"Look at all of those fish jumping. Where did the biggest fish go?" asked Dad.

"Eee-e-e-e-e-e-e-eeeek!"
screamed Mom. "Get this fish off
my lap!"

"Oh, no!" everyone groaned.

"Mom caught the biggest fish!"
said Matt.

Dad took the biggest fish from Mom's lap and held it over his head. "Guess what?" Dad shouted. "Mom won the fishing contest!"